She and Sea

Umama Munazha

Ukiyoto Publishing

All global publishing rights are held by

Ukiyoto Publishing

Published in 2023

Content Copyright © Umama Munazha

ISBN 9789360167028

All rights reserved.

No part of this publication may be reproduced, transmitted, or stored in a retrieval system, in any form by any means, electronic, mechanical, photocopying, recording or otherwise, without the prior permission of the publisher.

The moral rights of the author have been asserted.

This is a work of fiction. Names, characters, businesses, places, events, locales, and incidents are either the products of the author's imagination or used in a fictitious manner. Any resemblance to actual persons, living or dead, or actual events is purely coincidental.

This book is sold subject to the condition that it shall not by way of trade or otherwise, be lent, resold, hired out or otherwise circulated, without the publisher's prior consent, in any form of binding or cover other than that in which it is published.

This title is produced in Association with Pachyderm Tales

www.pachydermtales.com

ACKNOWLEDGEMENT

I whole heartedly thank,

Mohanasundari Jaganathan,

(Managing Director of Sharp Electrodes Pvt Ltd)

for funding this project.

Without her, this book would not be possible!

This book was a part of workshop conducted in our college, NGM College Pollachi and Pachyderm Tales.

I whole heartedly thank our management, our teachers and HOD of English Dept, NGM as well as Suja Mam for this initiative.

She and Sea

A lone girl is standing at a **seashore** as the sun is slowly setting.

She and Sea

The looming **darkness** of the dusk makes her think about her own darkness.

She and Sea 5

Her eyes start tearing up and no matter how hard she tries to ignore her inner pain and sufferings, it rather seemed impossible as the tears escape her dewy eyes.

She and Sea 7

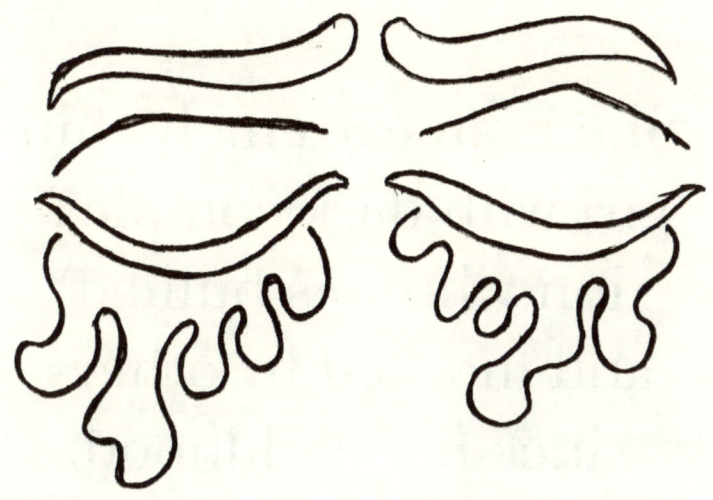

She is an extremely thin girl with dark complexion who was bullied and mocked by others since her childhood.

She and Sea

She has no friends to share her pain, thoughts, feelings and emotions. She bottled up everything inside her and now, she is like a rock, solid and hard in appearance but still a gem inside.

She and Sea

Then suddenly, she hears an unknown voice calling out for her from the sea.

She initially panics and later realises that it is the Sea Goddess, that's addressing her.

She and Sea

The Goddess starts saying that "I am loved and adored by most of the people."

She and Sea

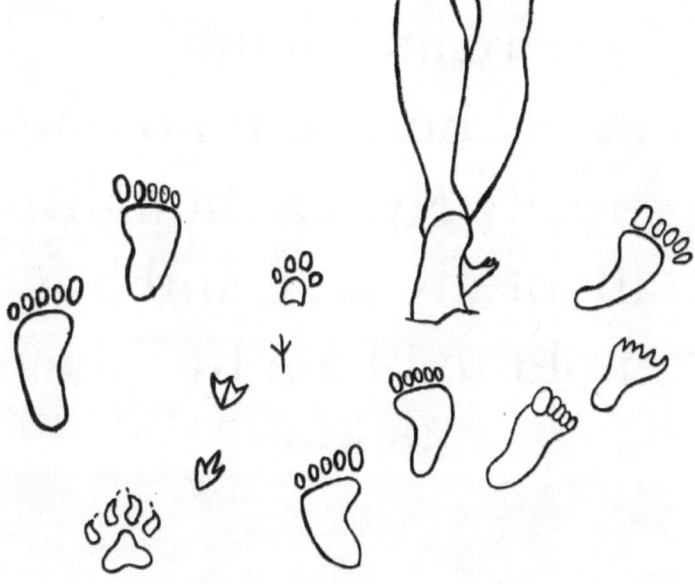

"Some visitors are often here and some are rarely here. But no one really gives a thought about my state and how polluted I am by their actions."

She and Sea

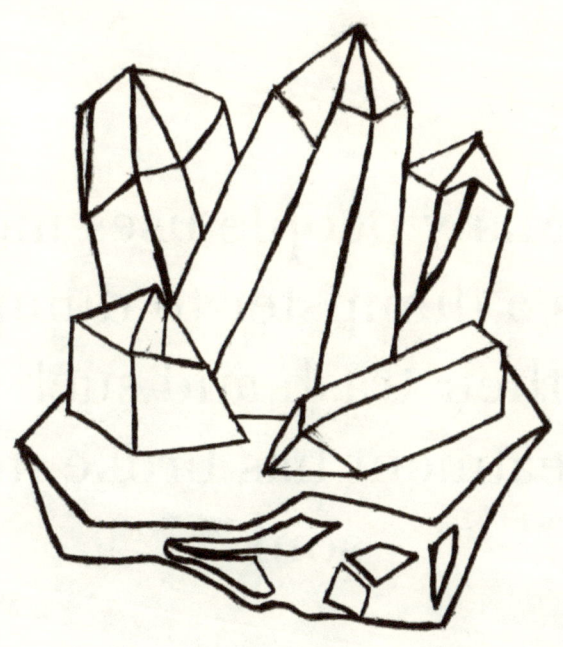

"Many people uses me as a dumpster to dump their trash and such treatment has broke my soul."

She and Sea

"We both might be two different beings but, we are the victims of the same people that mocks and disrespects us. They make me impure, unfit for the life that lives inside me".

After listening to this, the girl totally understands how the sea goddess is feeling and empathises with her.

She & Sea have the similar feelings and this made the girl to promise the sea that she will act on the pollution issue.

After that day, they both became very close friends and understood each other's pain because of their similar personalities and the girl helped Sea Goddess by Creating awareness about pollution.

The Author

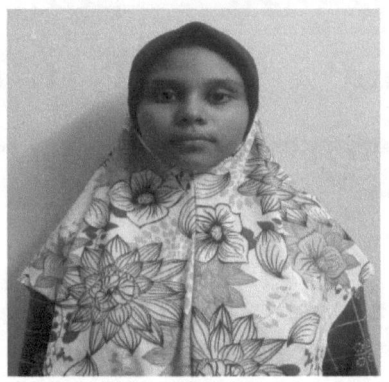

A. Umama Munazha is a final year graduate of English literature, studying at NGM college. She is a creator who is interested in illustrating and doodling. This is her first story and it is about the friendship of a little girl and the sea.

www.ingramcontent.com/pod-product-compliance
Lightning Source LLC
LaVergne TN
LVHW041643070526
838199LV00053B/3535